TAVON DOES IT ALL

WRITTEN BY: TAVON MASON with "MRS.ASHLEE" CHESNY

ILLUSTRATED BY: THOMAS BARNETT

Tavon Does It All

ISBN: 978-1-7338601-1-6

For bulk orders and author bookings
email tmason18@gmail.com.

"Believe, succeed and reach for the stars. Only you can stop your dreams from being real. Dare to Be Great!"

—Tavon Mason

Have more fun with Tavon after the story.
There is a special surprise in the back of this
book just for you!

Tavon was a football player. In fact, he was the best player on the Rams football team. But there was something even more special about Tavon. Soon his teammates would find out exactly what it was.

Tavon was always the first one to practice and the last one to leave. He scored the most touchdowns during the season, but he also helped his teammates become better football players. Whenever his teammates needed help with plays, Tavon would stay late after practice to help them.

Everyone knew that Tavon was especially kind. When his team lost a game, Tavon was sure to show great respect and sportsmanship. He would shake hand with the other team's players and tell them "good game". Then Tavon would keep his team motivated to work even harder to win the next game.

Tavon worked so hard at football, that all his teammates knew that Tavon would become a big-time football star. They all had the same dream. It was all they thought about and imagined. They believed that being a professional athlete was all that Tavon thought about too. But soon they would find out that there was more to Tavon than they could have ever known.

It was the day of the biggest game of the season: the championship game. The Rams were playing their rival team, The Chiefs.

The game announcers begin giving a play by play. "The Rams are down by two points. They have a 2nd down on the Chiefs' 20 yard line with just seconds left on the clock."

The Rams quarterback throws an incomplete pass to Tavon. "Tough break for the Rams! Anyone can see that the Rams are starting to feel the championship game slipping away."

The Rams coach, Coach Green, calls a timeout to talk to his team about the next play that they will run. "We're going to have to kick a field goal guys," he says. "We have a 3rd down with only 10 seconds left."

"But coach, we haven't made a field goal all season and we don't have a good kicker. Remember, Michael injured himself last year. Can't we just try a different play for Tavon to catch a pass for a touchdown?" asked John the quarterback.

Tavon told the team with excitement, "Russell can do it! He's an awesome kicker."

The team and Coach Green all look over toward their tall and skinny teammate who hasn't kicked for a field goal all season. Russell twiddles his thumbs and looks down at the laces on his cleats.

"Ah, man! We're going to lose!" John and the other teammates begin to complain with doubt.

"He can't do it!"

"Trust me, he can do it guys!" Tavon says.

"Ok, Tavon," Coach Green says. He looks toward Russell, "You're in, kid!"

Russell put on his helmet and looked at Michael wishing that he could do it instead. But then he took a breath and began to run out on the field with his teammates but quickly tripped over his own feet. The entire stadium laughed, but the Chiefs players laughed especially hard. The Rams began to shake their heads at their coach's decision.

Tavon helped Russell up and told him, "It's okay. You can do this! I know you can!"

Russell took a deep breath, and took his place behind the ball. The stadium was completely quiet. Russell got a great running start to the ball and BOOOOMMMMM!!!! Russell squeezes his eyes shut because he can't stand to watch where the ball goes.

"The Rams win the championship! The Rams win the championship!" The announcers scream with excitement.

The Rams were so excited and began to celebrate! Fans rushed the field cheering for the Rams' championship victory.

Coach Green told his team, "I am so proud of you all. This has been an amazing season with an unexpected hero! Get your things. I am taking you all out for pizza!"

The teammates high-fived each other, as they heard their bellies grumble with excitement.

When everyone met Coach Green back on the field, Tavon was missing. "Where is Tavon?" Michael asked.

Before anyone could answer, a big book came running through the tunnel from the locker room. It started to tell a great story with special voices for each character, "There once was a special girl named Kiya. With her best friend, Jaelynn, they did awesome things..."

Tavon's teammates' eyes grew big and their mouths hung open with surprise!

But then a report card came running out too. It read aloud, "Student name: Tavon Mason. Grade: 3rd.
Card marking: 1st. Teacher: Mrs. Robinson. Math: A. Language Arts: A. Science: B. Social Studies: B. Reading: A."

Tavon sprinted out of the tunnel trying to catch the book and report card. He was still in his uniform from the game. His teammates stood there watching it all happen. Coach Green was shocked too!

As Tavon ran after the book, out came a bunch of cartoon character slippers. "We are getting donated today," they said in their character voices. "We are going to special boys and girls at different children's hospitals."

Tavon gasped for air from running and thought to himself 'Geesh, there are too many things to catch.' Everything that he kept in his gym bag was now running across the football field. The book read stories, the report card read his grades and the cartoon character slippers were talking about getting donated to sick children.

Finally John asked Tavon, "Why do you have all these things with you?"

"These are the other things that are important to me," Tavon answered.

"You don't just play football?" TJ asked with surprise.

"No! I spend lots of time studying to have good grades. I love to read and I collect cartoon character slippers for sick kids in the hospital who are in need of a little joy," Tavon said with a big smile on his face.

Kameron looked down at his feet. "What's the matter?" Tavon asked.
"I only play football," Kameron said sadly.

"There are so many other things that you could do too. All you have to do is try some new things and pick what you like to do. It's never too late to start!" Tavon said. "You can even go with me to see if you like some of the things I do."

With a smile his face Kameron said, "You're RIGHT!"

Tavon's teammates helped him catch all of his things and then they went out for pizza. While they sat and enjoyed the pizza with Coach Green, they all talked to Tavon about other things they might like to try.

Coach Green smiled and said, "My team is so awesome!"

Russell smiled at the coach, less shy than ever before. "Yep, Coach! Like Tavon, we're going to do it all!"

Keep up with Tavon as he does it all!
www.tavonmasonlovesthekids.org.

TAVON DOES IT ALL

WRITTEN BY: TAVON MASON WITH ASHLEE CHESNY
ILLUSTRATED BY: THOMAS BARNETT

A Baltimore native, Tavon Mason has an impressive history with football, education and the community. Mason was standout at Woodlawn High School where he played tailback, defensive back and quarterback. He earned All-State, All-Metro, All-County and All-City honors and was chosen as his team's Most Valuable Player and team captain three times. He was inducted into the Woodlawn High School Scholar-Athlete Hall of Fame and participated in the Chesapeake Classic and the Mason-Dixon Shriner's All-Star Game.

Tavon was a standout at the University of Virginia, where he also earned his Bachelor's degree. Following his NFL dreams, he was signed as a rookie free agent by the New York Jets on Apr. 26, 2002. He spent the 2002 and 2003 training camp with the Jets, appearing in all eight preseason games, but was released following both.

Off the field, Mason is the CEO and founder of the Tavon Mason Loves the Kids Foundation to promote health, fitness, and education. He is also a paraeducator at Parkville High School and a part-time instructor at Trellis Services.

Keep up with Tavon and his organization at www.tavonmasonlovesthekids.org.

Ashlee Chesny known as "Mrs. Ashlee" is the founder of literacy nonprofit called Genius Patch and a 5x published children's author. She is an award-winning literacy advocate, as well as an advocate for woman and children of color. Learn more about her work and other books at www.geniuspatch,org.